CW00428784

It takes hours and hours to create and write the Bogsproggler stories, and it has been a tough road and I would just like to show my appreciation by giving a shout out to the following.

Thanks

Dad, Mum

Bro, Sis and the rest of our clan

Nan for always believing in me.

My City Watch - Nin, Bal, Tom, Jen, Mike (you owe me a Nando's.) Scan, Steph and the rest of the motley crew I call friends (you know who you are.)

Max dog, Max cat, Diddums Doodles (twice huh?), Pada, Smellan, Rosie, Kilmuff, Tish (Octo-pus), Julie and Rusty, Claire and Rob.

All my family and friends

And especially all my Boggles, everyone who has stuck by me and continues to. Thank you all.

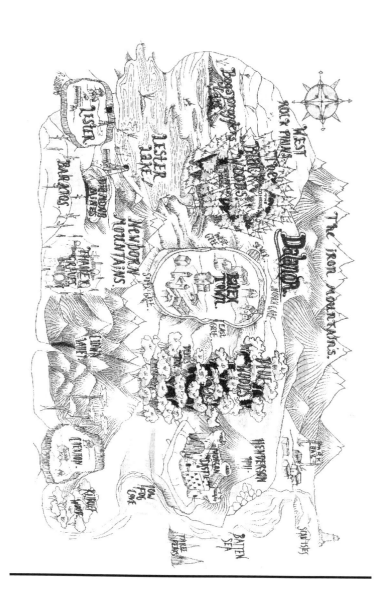

The Bogsproggler in Balen-Town

Chapter 1

A Tiptoe in the Shadow

The stars twinkle brightly above the city, a hundred thousand sparkling eyes watching over the land below. The air is cold and the crackle of the torches that light the pathways and walls of Balen-Town is all that can be heard in the dead of night. Two men of the City Watch, Smit and Bohdan, guard the West Gate. Smit sits on a makeshift stool crudely constructed from old beer crates while Bohdan leans lazily against the strong iron-bound gate. As they chat about the long night ahead, Smit looks up at his friend:

"Can't believe we pulled the night watch again. If you had only kept your mouth shut."

"Me? It was you who called the Captain a fool."

"I wasn't calling him a fool, I was calling you a fool. Now we have a whole week of night watches!"

"What did I do? It was you wh..."

"Shhh, what was that?" Smit bolts up from his stool and listens carefully.

Bohdan stands up straight. "What was what?"

"Thought I heard something from down there." He points at the drain in the cobbled road above one of the city sewers

"From the sewer? Nothing down there but rats, BIG nasty rats," says Bohdan, a puzzled expression on his face.

Smit sits back down and relaxes. "Yeah, you are probably right, just rats."

The sewer is dark and smelly. Water trickles from the ceiling in mini waterfalls. A pitter-patter of little webbed toes splash in the water, followed by another pair of slightly larger feet. After a while, the splashing stops. The young boy reaches into his pocket, rummages about for a few seconds and then pulls out a sheet of fire paper. Fire paper is a very flammable and sticky item that can be stuck onto almost anything. Once it sticks it will burn brightly for a long time. It's very dangerous and should be handled with extreme care. He presses the fire paper against the wall and it ignites, illuminating the sewer. Looking up at him with big wide eyes and a nervous smile is the Bogsproggler.

The boy stares at his new friend for a while without saying a word, trying to process what has just happened. He has never seen an odd-looking creature like this before, but he is not scared, he's fascinated.

"So, what are you?" he asks.

The Bogsproggler doesn't say a word and just stares back at the boy, he is also trying to figure out all that has happened so quickly.

"Can you not speak? You are a very odd-looking thing, aren't you?" The boy steps closer to the Bogsproggler and bends down to get a closer look at him.

The Bogsproggler looks at the bracelet on his wrist and remembers what the brothers told him just before he left the clearing. While wearing this bracelet, he can understand and speak any language. With slight hesitation, he replies shyly but cheerfully:

"I'm… I'm a Bogsproggler."

The boy laughs. "A Bogsproggler? You can't be, Bogsprogglers are tall, evil things with big red eyes and sharp claws, everyone in Balen-Town knows that."

The Bogsproggler looks down at his little webbed fingers and then back up at the boy.

"I don't have sharp claws. That sounds like the Jackal. He lives in the Black Woods. He was behind me when I fell into the stream."

The boy feels a little confused.

"I heard the Bogsproggler eats children and will attack anyone that walks in the Black Woods. No one has set foot in there for years."

"No, no, no!" The Bogsproggler squeaks. "I only like to eat moss, lots and lots of tasty moss. Unfortunately, it's all run out in my cave on Black Wood Marsh, that's why I'm here. I'm trying to get to the Blue Woods to find another cave filled to the top with moss." The

Bogsproggler explains to the young boy everything that had happened: the Guardians, the Jackal, the bracelet and the potion.

"Wow! That's amazing!" The boy, excited by what he has just heard, jumps about in the water. "This is great! Wow! A real live Bogsproggler here in Balen-Town."

Suddenly his face drops.

"Oh no."

Squeak squeak. "What's the matter?"

"Balen-Town doesn't take too kindly to non-humans. It's alright, I will help get you across to the other side of the city but not until tomorrow though. If my mother finds out I've snuck out again, I'll be grounded, forever!"

The Bogsproggler wiggles his toes in excitement. "Oh, thank you so much."

"Anything for a friend." The boy smiles at The Bogsproggler.

"Oh, by the way, I'm Isaac, pleased to meet you." Isaac extends his hand.

The Bogsproggler, never having shaken anyone's hand before, doesn't know what to make of this gesture. He stares at the hand for a few seconds then slowly sticks his little tongue out and licks it.

Isaac laughs "Haha eww."

The bashful Bogsproggler smiles back at him.

"Right, we better get back to my place, you can hide in my room until the morning and then we can set off."

The pair continue through the sewer, winding through the labyrinth of tunnels for what seems like hours until they come to a small opening in the wall. Isaac points towards the gap.

"This is my place, it will take us into the basement, then we just need to sneak upstairs and you can spend the rest of the night under my bed."

Isaac squeezes through the gap in the wall and up a small ramp into the basement. The Bogsproggler hesitates at first but trusts his new friend and follows.

Chapter 2

A New Day

As the sun rises, flocks of Nin birds descend from the mountains in the north singing in unison over the Balen-Town before settling in the treetops of the Black Woods to the west. There are four main entrances to the timber-walled city: the North Gate with its road to the Iron Mountains and beyond, the East Gate for the road to the Blue Woods and Devil's Drop then on to the Batten Sea, and, in the wealthiest southern quarter, the grandest gate on the road to the New Born Mountains, Clown Valley and Baralos. This gate is heavily guarded by the Knights of Balen-Town, elite hand-picked warriors led by the battle-hardened Captain Rikederf who also commands the City Watch. Lastly, there is the West Gate, looking out on The Black Woods and the road to Lester. This western quarter, Old Town, is the poorest consisting mainly of slums and run-down shops.

Just north of the city's centre stands a large and imposing mansion where the Mayor lives with his wife. They are a mean couple who care only about money and their own wellbeing. The Mayor long made out that he was there for the people of the city, but as soon as trouble started, or the people struggled to find the work that he promised, he would lock himself away in his mansion with his wife, where they would laugh at the less fortunate. Captain Rikederf does not see eye-to-eye with the Mayor due to a troubled past but works alongside him for the people of Balen-Town. The Captain is very caring and loyal to his city, and does everything he can to help its citizens knowing that the Mayor only looks out for himself.

Isaac and The Bogsproggler sneak slowly through the basement not knowing that it is now early morning, tip-toeing so they don't wake up Isaac's mother, Soer. As they near the bottom of the stairs leading up to the kitchen the Bogsproggler spots something familiar and tasty growing against the wall of the basement.

"Moss," he squeaks uncontrollably and hops over to the moss to start picking at it.

"Shhh, you'll wake up the whole of Balen-Town," says Isaac.

"Oops, sorry. I forgot." The Bogsproggler hangs his head.

"No problem. We will soon be in my room, just up the stairs, through the kitchen and it's on the other side of the hallway. Follow me… quietly."

They work their way up the creaky old wooden stairs. Each step cracks and groans as they climb slowly trying to stay as quiet as mice. Even though it was not really that loud, every step sounded like the roar of a Weboof.

Weboofs are odd creatures: small hairy fluff balls with big sharp teeth and a high-pitched roar. They can be tamed and become very useful pets. Due to their sharp teeth and speed, the people of Park Bay used them out in the fields, before the disaster. They would help gather crops and pick weeds. Though they are very cute looking they can give a nasty bite if provoked. Some say they are deadly if in a pack, though there is no evidence of this.

As Isaac opens the door to the kitchen, his mother, Soer, is standing there looking straight at him.

"And where have you been? It's dawn Isaac, you know it's not safe outside the walls after dark. Have you been out all night?" Soer wasn't angry at him for going out, just concerned for his safety.

"What is that?" She shrieks while pointing at the Bogsproggler, who is just standing there looking up at her, little webbed fingers tapping together and a smile on his face.

"Hello, I'm a Bogsproggler." He gives a little timid wave and starts backing slowly down the stairs.

"A Bogsproggler?" Soer, stunned and confused, steps back and sits down in her wooden chair.

"Mother, It's fine, he's friendly. I found him while outside playing in the river. I know I shouldn't have been there. He came out of the Black Woods. He was being chased by something, something big, with glowing red eyes and sharp claws. A Jackal. We have been in the sewers most of the night. The people of Balen-Town have got it wrong mum, it's the Jackal that attacks lonely wanderers in the wood, not the Bogsproggler."

"I need some water," says Soer, still wary of this odd-looking thing. The Bogsproggler hops up the stairs into the kitchen, up onto a stool and fills a goblet with water and hands it to Soer. She flinches as he approaches her. The Bogsproggler places the goblet next to her and then hops back behind Isaac. The three of them simply stare at each other in silence, trying to take in the situation. After finishing her water, Isaac's mother speaks sternly:

"Isaac, what are we going to do? You know Balen-Town has a strict human-only policy. They won't even let people have Weboofs as pets."

"Do not worry mother, I will try and sneak him out the East Gate or even the North Gate if need be."

The Bogsproggler approaches Soer. "Sorry, for the inconvenience. I don't mean to be any trouble. It's just I was being chased by the Jackal and Isaac helped me. I'll go back outside."

His face drops and, turning away, he slowly makes his way to the top of the stairs.

"Wait, come back little one. Why were you out in the Black Woods?" asks Soer.

The Bogsproggler explains all about his cave, the moss and how he needs to get to the Blue Woods, where hopefully there is a cave budding with all the moss he could ever need. He went on to explain about the Brothers and the Jackal and how his flight led him here. After hearing his story, Soer agrees to let Isaac help him reach the other side of town. Soer has a kind heart and is very accepting. She makes up a small bed next to Isaac's for the Bogsproggler and tells them both to get some sleep and they will work out how they will get the Bogsproggler across the city unseen after dark.

At the West Gate, Smit and Bohdan have fallen asleep propped up against the wall while waiting for the day watch to arrive. As they doze they are completely unaware that the Captain approaches.

"BOHDAN! SMIT! WAKE UP!"

They bolt upright and salute the captain.

"We weren't sleeping on the job sir," replies Bohdan.

"Sure weren't sir," adds Smit.

Both look a little sheepish, knowing they have been caught out but they try to act as if they had not done anything wrong. However, the Captain is not easily fooled. They have been together for a long time and have built up a solid reputation over the last few years and, having served the required two years, Bohdan and Smit are due to take their Knights of Balen-Town trial in three days' time.

"Smit, Bohdan, please try and focus, stay awake. You have your trial coming up soon. You're both good men, good soldiers, I would be proud to call you Knights of Balen-Town. But at this rate, falling asleep on the night watch, the lack of discipline... If you continue like this, you will not pass the trial. You are both fine swordsmen, two of the best this city has ever seen, so don't let me down. Here comes the day watch. Go home, get some rest and be ready for tonight's watch."

"Sir, yes Sir," they say in unison.

The Captain has a soft spot for Smit and Bohdan. They remind him of his own time in the City Watch. He gives a nod of acknowledgement and a faint smile as he dismisses them. As they head for home, the men of the day watch take over and the Captain sets out for the city centre and his regular morning meeting with the mayor.

Chapter 3

The Captain of Balen-Town

The Mayor stares out the window of his breakfast room overlooking Old Town in the distance.

"Look at them all, peasants," he scoffs, with an upturned nose and a look of disgust.

"Repulsive," snaps his wife Lady Valtine. She sits hunched over the table stuffing her face. "You need to find a way to get rid of this scum, darling."

The Mayor turns back to his wife, a sinister grin on his face.

"Yes, and I have just the plan. At the end of this week, I shall increase the Balen-Town Living Tax by twenty-five percent for anyone living in the west of the city and fifteen percent for the rest."

"Brilliant darling, absolutely wonderful news," she chuckles.

"It's simple my dear, more income for us, and less for everyone else. Most people in the city will be able to afford that and shall stay. But the scum in the west, the poor, the needy. Well... I'm afraid it will be the end of life in Balen-Town as they know it. Then, once the peasants have all gone we shall turn Old-Town into our second home using the money coming in from the tax increase." The Mayor begins to laugh with such malice it seems to fill the room with darkness. His wife joins in and they can barely contain themselves.

There is a knock at the door. They stop laughing and look at one another. The

Mayor stands motionless for a while, making whoever is at the door wait.

"Enter," he barks.

The door swings open. A servant, one of many, stands timidly in the doorway.

"The Captain of the City Watch and Knights of Balen-Town is here to see you, Sir." His voice trembles as he speaks.

"Hmm, fine, send him in."

The Captain storms in. He is not intimidated by the Mayor or his wife.

"Sir, My Lady, good morning. I have done as you asked and reduced the number of City Watch on the West Gate. As I said before, I feel this is a mistake and..."

The Mayor shouts and cuts him off:

"I don't care what you feel, Captain Rikederf! It is your job to do as I say." His face reddens.

Rikederf remains calm but stern. "My job, sir, is to keep the good people of this city safe by any means necessary, not to put them, my City Watch or the Knights at risk from potential attack just so you and your wife can fill your pockets."

"HOW DARE YOU!" shrieks the Mayor's wife. "We have nothing but good intentions for the people of Balen-Town."

The Mayor clears his throat and pipes up. "You come in here, you insult my wife and me. Who do you think you are, Captain?"

Rikederf stares him directly in the eye with such loathing that the Mayor looks away. "I know your intentions, and you know exactly who I am... Sir."

He turns and slams the door shut behind him.

Chapter 4

A Flawless Plan

In the kitchen, the Bogsproggler, Isaac and Soer sit around an old wooden table upon which a map of Balen-Town is spread. It is late afternoon and the sun is dipping below the rooftops. Soer has spent hours planning the safest route through Balen-Town using small stones placed on the map.

"Little Bogsproggler, if you follow this route you should be able to get out by the North Gate and then follow the road running south of the Iron Mountains for two days and that will bring you to the edge of the Blue Woods. The East Gate is just too far, and it will be hard to navigate through the city's streets."

The Bogsproggler's little eyes light up as his hand moves fast across the table and grabs one of the pebbles on the map. "MOSS."

He pops it in his mouth and smiles. Soer and Isaac look at him in mild reproach.

"That's the route little Bogsproggler," Isaac laughs. The Bogsproggler, looking slightly embarrassed slowly takes the small pebble out of his mouth. Now completely clean and moss-free and places it back.

"Oops, sorry. I can't help myself when it comes to moss."

"That's alright." Soer smiles. She can't help feeling a little bit sorry for him. Such an innocent and pure creature has had such a bad reputation for so many years when all this time it was the Jackal. She wonders if the Jackal drove the Bogsproggler and the rest of his kind into the caves all those years ago.

A knock at the door makes them all jump.

"Quick! Hide!" Soer says in a panic.

The Bogsproggler jumps down from his stool and runs around the kitchen looking for somewhere to hide, his little webbed toes slapping on the cold stone floor as the knocking becomes more insistent.

Isaac opens one of the cupboard doors. "Bogsproggler, quickly, in here, stay quiet."

The Bogsproggler gets into the cupboard and covers his mouth with his little hands as Soer walks to the front door. Isaac stands by the cupboard trying to act as natural as possible. He hears his mother open the door.

"Brother," she says surprised. "I've missed you, come in."

Captain Rikederf hurries into the kitchen. "Hello Isaac, my, how you've grown, you'll be able to join the City Watch soon."

Uncle and nephew hug each other having long had a special bond.

"Hahaha, it's good to see you boy."

In that unexpected moment, Isaac forgot about the Bogsproggler hiding in the cupboard.

Rikederf turns to Soer and explains how he thinks the Mayor is up to something and is targeting the poor in the west of the city. "Soer, you and Isaac need to get out of here, I don't know what he is planning, but it won't be nice. Please come stay with me in the Knight's Barracks."

"No Rikederf, we can't burden you with our problems; we will find a way I'm sure." Soer knows that if she and

Isaac were to move to the Knight's Barracks and the Mayor were to find out Rikederf could lose his job. "You have sacrificed so much to get to where you are."

"Then please, take this." He hands over a bag of gold coins. "That should be enough to help for a while, I will come back when I can with more."

"Thank you so much." With tears in her eyes, she embraces her brother.

"I must take my leave. The changing of the City Watch will be taking place in a few hours and there are a couple of men I need to make sure turn-up." Rikederf looks around the kitchen and smiles as he remembers his old family home when suddenly…

"What's that?"

From under a cupboard door, three little webbed toes are poking out. He walks towards the cupboard.

Soer and Isaac both shout:

"Don't!"

Rikederf flings the door open and there, with his hands over his mouth, is the Bogsproggler.

"Hi," he squeaks and gives a little wave.

"What is it?" Rikederf pulls his sword and points it at the creature.

The Bogsproggler recoils into the cupboard in fear as Isaac runs to protect his new friend. He stands between Rikederf's blade and the Bogsproggler.

"No, Uncle. Don't hurt him he's my friend. Please, I beg you, please."

"Out of the way Isaac. I must do my duty. Balen-Town is a human-only city."

"But why? It's not right. He hasn't hurt anyone he's just trying to find his way to a new home, just like you and mother did when you first came to the city as children." Isaac doesn't budge, he stares at his uncle just like Rikederf did with the Mayor earlier that day.

"Brother, please. Lower your sword, let me explain." Soer says calmly as she places her hand on his shoulder.

He steps back and places his sword back in its scabbard, eyes never leaving the Bogsproggler.

"Here, take this." Soer hands Rikederf some water, and he sits down at the table.

"It is safe little one, come out. He won't hurt you. Explain to Rikederf what you explained to me," said Soer.

The Bogsproggler emerges slowly and stands close to Isaac. He lets out a hesitant little squeak and clears his throat.

Several hours later and after many misunderstandings, Soer, Isaac and Rikederf are all engaged in conversation, thinking of the best way to help the Bogsproggler get out of Balen-Town when Rikederf stands.

"Sister, I must leave, night has fallen, and the changing of the guard is upon us. I shall come back after and help you get your little friend out of the city. You have two uses left of that invisibility potion, do you not?" He looks at the Bogsproggler and smiles.

Squeak squeak. "Yes, I do."

"Well if need be you can take that, then follow me to the gate in the north of the city." Rikederf stands up and walks to the door. "Just make sure you stay here and hidden until I return."

The door closes quietly behind him.

"Thank you so much. Isaac, thank you, Soer. I don't mean to cause you any trouble. I was planning to hop all the way around the outside of Balen-Town, but the Jackal was at the edge of the woods. Isaac saved my life. Thank you." Worry and sadness filled his eyes. "I hope the Brothers are OK."

Soer takes The Bogsproggler's hand. "I'm sure they are little one, I'm sure they are. Have hope, for hope is all we have."

Her voice instils confidence into The Bogsproggler's heart though they all know the reality may be very different.

Chapter 5

A Long Night

The sky burns a beautiful bright orange, with specks of fluorescent pink and dreamy yellow, as the sun sets behind the hills of the Black Woods. Smit and Bohdan walk along the winding cobbled streets of Old Town towards the West Gate. They play the game they always play while on any uneven surface. An easy and simple game of who can trip who up first, or as they call it, *Ground Pound*.

The rules for *Ground Pound* are very easy and anyone can play. All you must do is trip or push a friend over while walking, but they must be unaware that it is about to happen. If you are spotted getting ready to trip or push someone over, then you must forfeit and are not allowed another turn until the other person has made their attempt. If unobserved, you must shout "Ground Pound!" as loudly as you can, just before making your move or again the turn is forfeit.

Just ahead of them stands an abandoned inn, once teeming with life, music, food and happiness, now just a rotting shell of history and sadness. Broken barrels and crates lay strewn across the street. A once cared for and proud part of town, it has now become its own tomb.

Smit and Bohdan both grew up in Old Town and remember it when it was swarming with market stalls and merchants. They still try and make the most of the run-down streets.

Bohdan, blissfully unaware that Smit has fallen a few steps behind him, walks right by the smashed barrels. With an almighty cry that could wake the dead, Smit charges into Bohdan. His heavy mail hauberk adds to his already impressive bulk as he crashes into Bohdan's side with extreme force:

"GROUND POUND!"

"Arrrrr!" Bohdan lands in a heap, followed by Smit, already laughing.

"Smit you fool." Bohdan laughs too. "Ow! my ankle."

Smit gets up and dusts himself down, still chuckling. "Sorry Bohdan, but you have to admit that was one of the best Ground Pounds ever. Give me your hand."

He extends his hand out to help his friend back up to his feet. As soon as he, does Bohdan grabs hold and pulls so hard it feels like his arm is going to come out of its socket.

"GROUND POUND!" Bohdan laughs again as Smit crashes into the barrels and crates next to him. "Got ya, Hahaha."

"Hey, not fair, it's not the rules, that doesn't count."

Rikederf comes marching around the corner. "Smit! Bohdan! Why are on you the floor? Get up, get up."

Smit bolts up right away and Bohdan slowly follows and shakes off the pain in his ankle. In unison they say:

"Yes Sir, Sorry Sir."

Rikederf can't help but let out a little chuckle as he very well knew what they had been up to. He used to play Ground Pound when he was younger.

"Your Knights of Balen-Town trial has been moved forward to tomorrow, please don't let me down. Now come along. I'll walk with you to the West Gate."

The three of them march on, exchanging stories and laughing.

The two guards from the day watch salute the Captain as he approaches. Rikederf turns to Watchman Golud. He orders him to go up to the walkway and light the torches for the night watch.

As Golud climbs the ladder next to the gate, Rikederf turns to the other guard. "Anything to report Watchman Athal?"

"No Sir. It's been quiet all day. A few kids messing around in the river outside the walls but nothing out of the ordinary."

"Very good Watchman, make sure you get some rest at the barracks, you are dismissed."

Watchman Athal salutes the Captain once more and waits for Golud. Out of his sight, Smit and Bohdan are fooling about still trying to play Ground Pound.

Rikederf looks at the sky, a strange expression on his face as a sudden chill comes over him. "Quick, form up!"

Without hesitation Smit, Bohdan and Athal snap into action, falling in behind the Captain as all draw their blades.

"What is it, Captain?" Bohdan asks.

Rikederf steps forward and peers through the spyhole in the West Gate, into the darkness of the Black Woods.

"I'm not sure. Something doesn't feel right." He looks up at Golud on the walkway. "Golud, over there, the edge of the Black Woods, what do you see?"

"Nothing Sir, I don't see anything." He strains his eyes against the flare of the nearest torch

"Are you sure man?"

"Positive, sir."

Rikederf lowers his sword. "At ease men, false alarm."

They relax slightly but know all too well that the Captain's instincts are usually right.

"Wait, Sir... I do see something. At the edge of the woods." Golud walks along the wall and leans over pointing towards the treeline.

Without warning, a dark clawed hand with razor sharp blades for fingers reaches over the wall and pierces his chest plate armour with ease. Golud lets out a blood-curdling scream and is pulled over the parapet. Rikederf spins around, his sword raised, he looks to where Golud had stood. In the darkness, he sees a large dark figure clumsily climbing over the wall, with glowing red eyes and cruel fingers as sharp as the finest sword, snapping its teeth and growling.

The Jackal.

"WATCHMEN AT ARMS." Smit, Bohdan and Athal fall back into formation. Athal calls for his friend.

"Golud, where are you?"

"Quiet, Athal, he's gone, stand fast." snaps the Captain, staring at the creature that stands on the walkway.

Its eyes glow red with hatred as it sneers down at them. It lets out a terrifying roar and throws its arms up into the air. A sound like a thousand knives striking and gouging fills the night, and atop the wall of Balen-Town, a seemingly endless row of red eyes appears.

Rikederf steps back and his face drops. Smit, Bohdan and Athal all look at each other with fear filled eyes, they have never seen anything like it, and they have never seen the Captain seem so lost.

Rikederf snaps out of his trance and starts barking orders:

"Athal, sound the horn, quickly man." Rikederf's voice carries the faintest of tremors. "Smit, Bohdan, rally to me!"

More of the creatures climb over the wall, dropping down to filter into the city's narrow streets, like rats into a sewer. Screams from men, women and children can already be heard as the beasts slice their way through the outskirts of Old Town. Athal runs as fast as he can towards the large iron horn mounted opposite the gate. There is one in each district for calling the Knights of Balen-Town and the City Watch in emergencies. He places his mouth to the horn and blows. A beautiful yet haunting sound cuts through the night sky. At once, other horns reply, one by one, each with its own unique sound, carrying the alarm across the city, shaking it awake.

Before the West Gate, Rikederf and his small party are poised ready for action. Five Jackals stand growling before them.

The Bogsproggler jumps out of his seat at the sound of the horns.

"What was that?" he squeaks.

Isaac looks at Soer. "Mother."

Soer runs to the window and looks out at Old Town's chaos: people run down the street crying, arming themselves with whatever they can find, everyone tripping over one another and running in different directions in the confusion. A large black figure rushes past the window and Soer screams. Another runs past and then another.

"The Jackal!" cries the Bogsproggler, hopping over to Soer and grasping her hand. "It's a Jackal, we need to go, NOW!

Quick, we need to hide." Isaac opens the door to the basement and the three of them run inside, slamming the door shut behind them.

In the darkness, Soer lights a candle. "What is it doing here? Did the Brothers not kill it?" Squeaks the Bogsproggler

"We can escape through the sewers," says Isaac.

"No, we need to stay put and wait for your uncle, he will know what to do. Who knows what it's like in the sewer or rest of the city." Soer whispers

The Bogsproggler sits down on the cold basement floor.

"There's more than one Jackal?" he mumbles, thinking of the struggle he and the Brothers had against just one in the clearing. "What are we going to do?"

Chapter 6

The Fight for Old Town

The Jackals charge. Rikederf raises his shield as razor-sharp claws lash at his face. Quick as a flash he sidesteps, bringing his sword down with such force, it cuts clean through the outstretched limb. The creature recoils, spouting foul ooze from the wound. Rikederf lifts his sword, and with a mighty swing, takes off the Jackals head.

Smit, Bohdan and Athal fight furiously, using every technique they have been taught to help defend themselves against the hideous monstrosities. Athal blocks a Jackals every strike as it swipes at him frantically. As the Jackal tires, Athal pushes the beast back before a sharp blow to the leg sends it crashing to the ground.

"Captain, I did it!" He glances briefly at Rikederf as more Jackals swarm over the wall.

"Athal, look out!" Rikederf cries, but it's too late. The wounded Jackal launches itself forwards, sharp claws slicing into Athal's torso. He stands motionless for a second before dropping his sword and falling to the ground.

"ATHAL!" Rikederf rushes to his aid and drives his blade deep into the creature's skull and it falls lifeless to the ground. Smit and Bohdan scream a war cry and go into a rage, hacking down Jackals heedless of their plight. Master swordsmen from a young age they fight on as Rikederf kneels by Athal's side.

"I'm sorry sir, I thought I had him."

"Such valour and selflessness, Balen-Town is forever in your debt, no need to be sorry." He takes the Watchman's hand. Athal looks to the stars and smiles, closing his eyes for the last time.

A Jackal closes on Rikederf from behind, mouth snarling and teeth oozing with drool, the Captain apparently unaware of the imminent danger, still holding Athal's hand. Letting out a fierce cry, he takes Athal's sword from next to the lifeless body and leaps to his feet, swinging two blades like a giant pair of shears, taking the Jackal's head clean from its shoulders. He stands, breathing heavily, swords by his side dripping with the dark putrid blood of his foe, taking in the chaos around him before going into his own fury and cutting down everything in his path. A line of slain Jackals lay across the street in the wake of the frenzied attack. Suddenly a deafening crash fills the air.

"Captain, the West Gate is breached," cries Bohdan, fending off multiple Jackals. The wood and iron of the gate shatters and like a flood, a host of Jackals pour through.

"Smit, Bohdan, fall back, rally to me!" bellows the Captain, still swinging both swords in a wild hypnotising display of steel. They retreat, slowly backing off while still facing the tide of monsters, for they know if they turn their backs, they will be cut down in an instant. Outnumbered two hundred to one, the reality of the situation is clear on everyone's face, but Rikederf is not one to bow down and surrender even when the odds are against him.

"Smit, Bohdan. It's been an honour, men, you truly are Knights of Balen-Town. Be brave, even in the face of death, do not let them see your fear and you shall win this day."

"SIR, YES SIR!" They cry.

"We are with you Captain," shouts Smit.

"Until the end, Sir," adds Bohdan.

"Very good, very good indeed." Rikederf smiles menacingly at the approaching wall of Jackals and holds his bloodied sword aloft. "Men of Balen-Town… Charge."

At that moment, a haunting yet beautiful sound resonates through the stricken streets.

"The Knights, the Knights of Balen-Town," Smit cries.

The sound of the Knights' horns stops the Jackals advance for an instant. From the streets of Old Town beyond the gate, one hundred glowing points hover like fireflies, waiting to be released and set free into the night. Somewhere in the darkness, a voice shouts:

"FIRE!"

A hailstorm of fire arrows rushes over Rikederf, Smit and Bohdan straight into the approaching Jackals, followed immediately by a roar of clashing steel and cheering. Once again from the darkness, a voice echoes:

"Knights, Charge!"

The Knights of Balen-Town appear, out of the darkness. Two hundred of the finest Knights in the land hurl themselves upon the enemy, swords, axes, spears, maces and halberds glinting in the torchlight.

"Sergeant Hammlin, so good to see you!"

"We came as soon as we could Captain Rikederf."

"Thank you, Sergeant, now let us take back our city from these repulsive demons."

Hammlin, a fearless and battle-hardened warrior, nods to the captain and continues onward into the fight.

The clash of iron and steel, teeth and claw, rages on, both sides searching for a victory. Shields shatter, swords swing, bones break. Howls from the Jackals and cries of soldiers ring out as the Knights fight to hold the line.

In the thick of the fight, Rikederf, after felling another beast, suddenly stops. Frightened for Soer, Isaac, and the Bogsproggler.

"Smit, Bohdan, follow me, quickly." Rikederf knows that his second in command is more than capable of holding off the faltering foe.

"Sergeant Hammlin, hold the line, reinforcements will be here soon. We are going to help the families in town."

Hammlin cuts down a Jackal, "No problem Captain, we've got this."

Rikederf, Smit and Bohdan run down a narrow street deeper into Old Town.

Chapter 7

No Time Like the Present

The Bogsproggler's little face lights up as he has an idea. "Soer, Isaac, why don't you both take some of my invisibility potion? I'm smaller and faster than humans and Jackals. I can go through the sewer and meet you outside the city."

Isaac is scared he may not see his new friend again. "No, we must stick together."

Soer agrees. "Isaac is right, little Bogsproggler we should stick together, and wait for Rikederf."

A loud banging on the door makes them all jump.

"Uncle Rikederf," says Isaac as he jumps up to open the door.

"Isaac, wait!" shouts Soer.

Isaac does not listen to his mother and continues up the staircase to open the door. As quick as lighting, the Bogsproggler rushes up the stairs and grabs Isaac's hand as he reaches for the handle.

"Isaac, wait. Listen, do you hear that?"

"No, I can't hear anything."

Bogsprogglers have very sensitive hearing, much better than humans and can pick up on the smallest of things when they pay attention.

"That's not a human breathing," squeaks the Bogsproggler. "Quick, get back."

As Soer waits anxiously and the Bogsproggler and Isaac race back down the stairs, a large, fearsome hand crashes through the door, its blade-like fingers searching for a victim.

Grumble grumble "Quick! Soer, Isaac take the potion! You must, I'll manage. The Brothers said they hadn't given it to humans, but no time like the present. Quick take a sip each."

The Bogsproggler gives the small bottle to Soer who takes a cautious sip before handing it to Isaac as the door splinters. Isaac fumbles around in his pockets, frantically looking for something. He pulls out some fire paper.

"Here, take this, it will help light the way, follow the sewer north and we shall meet you outside the North Gate."

"Isaac look, it's working." Soer whispers.

The potion turns them both transparent and, just before fading from view, Soer smiles at the Bogsproggler. "We will be there little one, now go, run."

The door bursts apart and a Jackal comes down the stairs, panting heavily, eyes fixed on the Bogsproggler. It raises its claws towards him ready to swipe. Soer and Isaac, now completely invisible, use this moment to their advantage.

Together, they run at The Jackal, knocking it down, then race up the stairs, leaving only the disturbed dust of their footsteps. While the Jackal is still stunned, the Bogsproggler dashes to the back of the basement and through the gap down into the sewer. The Jackal now close behind cannot fit through and flails its arm wildly, attempting to grasp his prey.

Quick as his little feet will carry him, the Bogsproggler runs into the darkness.

Chapter 8

Alone Again

It is cold and intimidating in the dark sewer, especially for someone as small as the Bogsproggler. After walking for a long while, the tunnel comes to an end in some larger space. He pulls out a piece of fire paper and sticks it to the wall. It catches fire and illuminates a labyrinth of tunnels. Numerous passageways run off in all directions from the underground chamber.

"Which way do I go?"

There are faint symbols carved above each tunnel which mean little to the Bogsproggler, the work of the men and women who built the sewers many years before his birth, pointing the way to certain districts within Balen-Town. For many years, thieves used these tunnels to escape capture from the City Watch and get to places that would normally be inaccessible via the city streets but now they are mostly long forgotten.

The Bogsproggler sits down and basks in the glow from the fire paper, trying to work out which path will lead him to the North Gate and out of the city. Movement in the tunnel he has just emerged from catches his eye. The glare from the fire paper restricts his vision and the figure is hard to make out. It moves slowly, hunched over and seems to be swaying from side to side. Whoever it is, it seems to be in distress and in pain. The flame from the fire paper starts to diminish as the Bogsproggler sees who or rather what it is…

A Jackal!

Even though it's near death it would still be able to harm the Bogsproggler if he is not careful. It stumbles into the gallery and sees him. Its eyes light up and it shrieks as the Bogsproggler jumps back and looks for something, anything, he can use to defeat it.

He looks at his wrist and remembers the bracelet and Brother Green's words when he handed it to him:

"Wear it and you will be able to speak and understand any language."

Despite his fear, the Bogsproggler looks at the Jackal moving towards him and lets out a squeak. "Stop."

The Jackal does exactly as commanded. Its eyes widen, looking at this small odd creature and it replies with a single word:

"Death."

"Death? What do you mean, why are you here, what do you want?"

The Jackal shuffles closer and closer to the Bogsproggler. "Death."

The Bogsproggler reaches for a piece of fire paper and grips it tightly.

"Please stop, don't make me do this." *Squeak grumble.*

Bogsprogglers are peaceful creatures. They do not like to fight, they like to help, but when faced with a life or death situation they will do what is necessary to protect themselves.

Once more he shouts. "What do you want?"

The Jackal, now only a few feet away looms over him and points. "Your soul, the last remaining soul of the creatures they call Bogsprogglers, your time has come, now die!"

It pulls its arms back ready to attack but the Bogsproggler throws the fire paper onto the Jackal's chest and it bursts into flames. The Jackal flails and roars, fleeing down the tunnel it came from before collapsing onto the cold, wet floor. Shocked, the Bogsproggler stands in silence a moment before running as fast as he can down the nearest passageway.

He runs and runs and doesn't stop, even passing moss-covered stones along the way. Twists and turns lead him ever deeper into the maze. At last, he comes to another junction, stopping to catch his breath and realising he is now utterly lost. His eyes, accustomed to caves, dimly make out two tunnels ahead.

"Oh no, what do I do?" he grumbles. "One of these must lead out of the sewer."

From the tunnel on the right, something blows out and lands on his webbed feet.

"Moss." He squeaks excitedly and gobbles it right up, then he notices something else.

"A breeze! This must lead out of the sewers, I did it." With a playful hop and almost forgetting everything that has happened, he scuttles off down this new tunnel towards the source of the breeze.

After a short distance, he finds a small opening high in the tunnel wall with a faint engraving, crudely etched above. If the Bogsproggler could read he would see the word, "Jackpot."

He enters through the opening, climbing up a narrow passage hacked long after the sewer builders finished their work, and then down a slope. He finds himself just above the base of a small dry well. A ladder leads up towards a wooden cover. Torchlight shines faintly between its rough planks.

"The North Gate?" he thinks.

At the top of the ladder, the cover is loose and easy to move. Carefully, while trying to balance on his little webbed toes, he pushes it open and hops out of the well.

"This doesn't look like the North Gate"

He stands in a large and beautiful garden, blossoming with all kinds of flowers. A long gravel track leads to an impressive looking mansion. Tall statues tower over the Bogsproggler, previous Mayors and Lords of Balen-Town, captured in beautiful stonework for posterity. A parade of torches lights the path towards the mansion.

"Wow!" squeaks the Bogsproggler. He has never seen anything so magnificent in all his life. His eyes widen with excitement as he starts to hop down the path. As he proceeds, he scans the ground for moss. Even at a time like this, there's always time for moss. Ahead of him, in front of the mansion, two guards patrol. He quickly jumps behind one of the statues and peers round to keep track of their movements.

"I need to get to the North Gate, there must be a sign around here somewhere" He scratches his head while thinking of the best possible way out. While rattling his brain about how to get to the exit he is unaware of two more guards who have appeared behind him.

"Don't move!" the first one shouts.

The Bogsproggler stands stiffly as he feels the tip of cold steel on his back. He lets out a squeak and puts his little webbed hands into the air.

"Please don't hurt me, I'm just looking for a way out. The Jackals are coming."

He turns around slowly to face the guards, both with swords drawn and pointing at the little Bogsproggler.

The taller of the two turns to someone standing in the shadows. "We have him Mayor Hanismiks."

The Mayor of Balen-Town appears, hands clasped together, a terrifying smile on his face.

"What have we here?" he hisses. "Guards, take him inside."

A net is thrown over The Bogsproggler. He struggles and lets out a cry for help. The guards scoop him up and head towards the grand doors of the mansion. The Mayor follows behind, his robes blowing in the wind. As he enters the doorway he swings round to one of his men stationed there.

"Get me Captain Rikederf, tell him I have found the creature attacking the city."

The doors slam shut behind him.

Chapter 9

Missing?

Rikederf bursts through the door of Soer's kitchen, both swords at the ready and runs frantically from room to room.

"Soer! Isaac! Soer!" His cries go unanswered but, as he returns to the kitchen where Smit and Bohdan have followed, a low growl comes from the basement.

"Captain, what was that?" asks Bohdan.

"Look! The door to the basement." Smit points his blade towards the smashed door and without hesitation, Rikederf hurries down the stairs.

"Captain!" Smit follows.

"Wait for me." Bohdan runs after his friend.

The Jackal is still reaching deep into the gap in the wall for the Bogsproggler. It turns around and sees Rikederf at the foot of the stairs. He charges, swinging both blades towards its head but miscalculates by a fraction of a second, receiving a powerful backhand to the chest, sending him flying onto the floor. Rikederf scrambles to pick himself up but loses his footing as the Jackal closes in.

"Away foul creature!" Smit runs at the Jackal, thrusting his sword towards its heart, and tries to pierce the tough hide of its torso, but it dodges to one side, the blade only nicking the beast's arm, leaving him trapped between the Jackal and the wall. The Jackal turns its attention away from Rikederf as Smit backs up, holding his sword by both hands at arms' length. The Jackal snaps at him with its jaws.

Bohdan, following down the stairs, hauls Rikederf up before throwing his sword to the floor and looking directly into Smit's eyes. "Brace yourself."

Smit nods in recognition, never taking his eyes from his foe as Bohdan launches himself.

"GROUND POUND!"

Bohdan slams into the Jackal's back sending it flying onto Smit's outstretched sword. The beast slumps to the floor, its glowing red eyes fading to black as it lets out its last breath.

"One all." Smit chuckles. Bohdan can't help but laugh, He extends his hand to help him up.

"Great job men, well done. They aren't here, but I know where they will be. Follow me." Rikederf heads back up the staircase into the kitchen. Smit and

Bohdan shake themselves down and rush up the stairs.

The streets are filled with panic and fire, fear and screams, as the people flee from Old Town. Through the smoke and chaos, Rikederf, Smit and Bohdan run toward the barracks.

"I'm sure Soer and Isaac made it out, Sir," Smit pants as they rush along the old cobbled streets.

"Captain, why are we heading to the barracks?" Asks Bohdan "The fight is in Old Town."

"I told them if they ever needed me, to go to the barracks, so that is where we are heading. Also, who knows what state the barracks are in, they may need our help."

They keep up the fast pace, almost making the whole way without running into any trouble.

The fight is no longer contained within Old Town, seeping into other areas of the city. Jackals tear at doorways trying to break into houses. The last of the Knights arrive to take back the streets. Pockets of resistance form, the people of Balen-Town start to fight back: farmers, blacksmiths, bards and shopkeepers all join ranks with the Knights, picking up anything they can use as a weapon to drive back this evil foe.

"For Balen-Town!" echoes around the streets. Passion and fearlessness consume the people as they fight for their freedom, their families, their very lives.

A small child no older than seven runs crying down a narrow alleyway pursued by a Jackal. Smit and Bohdan immediately change course, Bohdan turning to Rikederf and calling out:

"We will catch up you up Sir, go find Soer and Isaac."

Rikederf nods and continues towards the barracks alone.

At the end of the alley past sturdy locked doors, a high wall blocks the girl's way. She cries out for help and curls up in a ball on the floor, as the Jackal snarls and drools. Smoke from nearby fires hangs in the air, filling the narrow space lit by a single spluttering torch. Like a ghost, Smit appears and bows before the creature, dropping down to one knee. Fast as a speeding arrow, Bohdan rushes through the smoke, a razor-sharp throwing dagger in each hand. At full speed, he places one foot on Smit's back and launches himself high into the air, throwing both daggers down towards the Jackal. They catch the light, gliding like two silver winged birds from the Iron Mountains. Smit is on his feet charging with his sword before the daggers strike hitting the Jackal in each shoulder, sending the beast's arms flying back. The creature lets out a fearsome screech as Smit's blade pierces its chest.

Smit kneels at the girl's side, taking her in his arms. "It's alright little one, you're safe now."

"Oh, thank you, thank you. When I grow up, I want to be a knight just like the two of you."

Bohdan retrieves the daggers from the Jackal's body, wiping the dark ooze from them and sheathing them on his belt. He draws his sword, at once wary and watchful. As they leave the alleyway, a man and woman rush towards them.

"Mother!" shouts the girl and runs to the approaching woman.

The girl's father approaches them. "Thank you so much, true Knights of Balen-Town, this will not go unheard, you truly are heroes."

Smit and Bohdan can't help but smile as the family enter a nearby house.

"Wow! That was incredible," sighs Smit.

"It sure was." Bohdan points down the road. A pair of Jackals lurk in the smoke. "Looks like we're up again."

The two friends draw their blades once more. They smile as they step forward.

Only a few men remain at the barracks when Rikederf arrives. Watchmen stand either side of the entrance, their spears crossed. As the Captain approaches, they part their spears and salute him and swing the doors open. The Captain hastens along the short corridor to the heart of the barracks: a large circular room with a long table at its centre and the Balen-Town crest proudly displayed above a large open fire. Two Watchmen stand before the door leading to the inner chambers. Having found sanctuary, Isaac and Soer sit at the table eating soup.

"Soer, Isaac." Rikederf almost breaks into a run. "I thought I'd lost you. What happened? We went to your house and found only a Jackal. Where is our little friend?"

Soer looks up at her brother solemnly and tells him how the Bogsproggler had given them the potion that helped save their lives, putting them before himself and of the promise made to meet him at the North Gate.

Rikederf briefly mulls this new information. "Very well, we will look for him as soon as the city is declared safe,"

A Watchman walks into the barracks, he approaches the Captain and salutes.

"Captain Rikederf, the Mayor requests your presence right away."

"I have a battle to win, tell the Mayor he will have to wait!"

The young soldier shuffles nervously. "But sir, the Mayor said it was a direct order. He said to tell you he has captured one of the creatures."

"Captured?" Rikederf cannot conceal his puzzlement.

"Yes, Sir."

"Very well, tell him I'm on my way." Rikederf dismisses the Watchman, turning his attention back to Soer and Isaac. "I must do this, but you wait here until I return and then I shall take you to the North Gate to find your friend."

"But uncle, the Mayor's house is on the way to the North Gate. Please take us with you."

"Isaac, it's too dangerous, I can't. You will make a fine Knight one day my boy, but today is not that day."

The barracks' horn sounds three times. Rikederf straightens up facing the door. Sergeant Hammlin enters, followed closely by Smit and Bohdan, and two dozen Knights assemble outside, broad smiles upon their faces.

Hammlin stands to attention. "Captain Rikederf, we have held the city; the last of those demons are being cut down as we speak. The Knights are going from street to street and rooting out the last of them."

"Remarkable work Hammlin, come in and rest. You have done the city a just service tonight, and you shall be rewarded for it." The Captain places his hands on Hammlin's shoulders and smiles. To have a high-ranking officer place his hands upon the shoulders of a subordinate is the sign of highest respect within the Knights of Balen-Town.

Hammlin steps back and salutes his Captain. "Thank you, Sir, but you know me. I can't rest until the threat is dealt with, I would like to remain out in the field until the situation is completely resolved."

"Of course, Sergeant, of course."

"These two Knights saved multiple lives and destroyed many beasts, we would not be here if not them for them." He gestures towards Smit and Bohdan who stand to attention just inside the doorway. "They are more deserving than any in tonight's victory."

"But we are only City Watch Sergeant Hammlin," mumbles Smit. Hammlin nods to the Captain.

Rikederf approaches Smit and Bohdan, he faces them and places his right hand on Smit's right shoulder and his left on Bohdan's left. "Welcome, Knights of Balen-Town." The Knights gathered outside the chamber erupt in cheers. Overwhelmed and hardly able to believe they are now Knights of Balen-Town, Smit and Bohdan grin at each other. before joining their new comrades in celebration.

"The city is safe, please may we come with you?" Isaac looks up at his uncle.

"Very well Isaac. Smit, Bohdan, you will help me escort young master Isaac and his mother, Lady Soer. There may still be a few of those creatures around, so we will move swiftly and quietly to the

Mayor's house to see this thing he has captured, then on to the North Gate."

"Sir, yes Sir."

Hammlin details half of his men and returns to the streets. Rikederf orders the remainder to get some well-deserved rest, as Soer and Isaac ready themselves.

He surveys Smit and Bohdan, both bursting with pride.

"Well then Knights, shall we?"

The five of them set out for the Mayor's mansion.

Chapter 10

Friend or Foe?

By the light of a window in the meeting hall, Mayor Hanismiks and Lady Valtine regard the cage intended for their prized falcons with disdain. Four men at arms, loyal to the mayor, are stationed around it. The Bogsproggler sits in the cage, his little webbed hands covering his eyes as he cowers, shivering with fear.

Lady Valtine bends down and sneers. "Eugh, what a repulsive little creature, what is it?"

"Disgusting is what it is my dear, disgusting." snorts the Mayor.

Lady Valtine then notices the bracelet on the Bogsproggler's wrist. "It's got jewellery on, Hanis my dear, it probably stole it from me. You there, bring it to me." A rough looking man-at-arms reaches into the cage and grabs the Bogsproggler's arm pulling it so hard he lets out a whimper. He removes the bracelet and hands it to Lady Valtine.

"Huh, it's rubbish, no value at all." She tosses it into the cold fireplace.

The Bogsproggler can no longer speak their language, letting out multiple squeaks and noises to no avail. *Squeak squeak, grumble, mumble.*

He reaches for the bracelet, but the fireplace is too far away. He sinks to the bottom of the cage and begins to cry.

"Pathetic creature," scoffs the Mayor. He laughs and points at the Bogsproggler.

Lady Valtine and the guards join in as one throws an old cloth over the cage plunging the Bogsproggler into darkness.

The doors at the far end of the meeting hall swing open, Rikederf stands at the head of his small party.

"Mayor Hanismiks."

"Captain Rikederf, do come in, won't you? And who are these peasants you have brought with you? A woman, a boy and two of the City Watch. This isn't a tavern Captain, this is a house of excellence."

"With all due respect Mayor, these are the two finest swordsmen of the Knights of Balen-Town, along with Lady Soer and her boy Isaac."

The Mayor stares at Soer, making her feel uneasy. "Oh, so this is sister Soer? Such a pity what happened to your father, wasn't it? If it wasn't for his untimely death, I wouldn't be Mayor. Do come in."

Soer's fists clench as she stares back at Hanismiks. "Thank you."

Rikederf's hand moves automatically, tightening around the hilt of his sword. "Mayor Hanismiks, why have you called me here? Did you not hear the horns of Balen-Town? Did you not see the smoke, the fire the pain and suffering? We have been fighting throughout the night. We have lost good men, while you sit behind your walls laughing and drinking."

"I know Captain, we also have been defending ourselves from these horrendous creatures all night, haven't we dear?"

"That's right, and while you had to call out the Knights of Balen-Town to clean up such a puny bunch of creatures, we managed to capture one, alive." Lady Valtine waves her hand to the cage situated behind them.

The Mayor beckons. "Come forward, look at this repugnant beast."

The party move cautiously into in the room and up to the cage. The Captain signals that Smit and Bohdan to be ready to attack, if it gets out. Isaac stands with his mother grasping her hand.

"Show it." The Mayor commands.

The cloth is pulled back and lying helplessly on the floor of the cage is the Bogsproggler, still shaking with fear.

"Bogsproggler!" Isaac cries as he darts towards the cage. "Let him out."

Isaac shakes the cage trying to set his friend free.

"Not so close you idiot." The Mayor reaches down and grabs Isaac by the wrist and pulls him away.

"Unhand him this instant." Soer rushes forward. The Mayor, without hesitation, strikes out with his free hand sending her sprawling on her hands and knees.

"Mother!"

"Stop!" Rikederf withdraws his blade, pointing it at Hanismiks' chest.

Smit and Bohdan are the first to react, drawing their own blades an instant before the mayor's men, Bohdan brandishing his twin daggers, Smit his short sword.

"Captain, I do believe you have made a mistake. Now be a good peasant and put down your weapon. Before I have you stripped of your title." The Mayor speaks calmly.

"Touch her again, and I will kill you, you have my word."

"Oh my, my dear Captain, you are in no position to say such things. All I wanted was to show you the creature we found and ask your opinion."

"And where did you capture this dangerous beast?"

"It was found wandering the gardens, close by the well."

"Hanismiks, this is not what we have been fighting all night. This is a Bogsproggler, he's just lost and trying to find his way home."

"A Bogsproggler? No, no Captain, Bogsprogglers are tall horrible creatures, with red eye and sharp claws." The Mayor snorts in derision.

"I beg to differ. You describe the creatures we have been fighting all night. We got it wrong. All this time, all these years. It wasn't the Bogsprogglers that threatened Balen-Town, but something else."

The Mayor's face drops. "What do you mean, those are what you have been fighting all night? Not these little green blobs?"

"Many of my men have died in the bitter struggle."

Lady Valtine moves to the window and looks out into the darkness. She turns to Rikederf. "Preposterous. You cannot fight myths. You're a fool, Captain, just like your father."

Rikederf confronts her, his sword still readied. "Lady Valtine, you know nothing of my father, he was a great man, a great leader. He cared for the people of Balen-town, he was selfless. Unlike yourself."

Valtine shakes with anger and cannot contain herself. "Hanismiks, kill them as you did his father."

"You killed our father?" The sword is lowered and Rikederf's face drains of colour.

Soer still on her knees sobs as Isaac clings to her. Smit and Bohdan stand firm waiting on their captain's word as the

Bogsproggler watches helplessly from the cage.

"Oh, I am truly sorry Captain, now you know the truth, we can't allow any of you to leave alive, so you will be executed along with this so-called Bogsproggler. Take them away." The Mayor speaks to Smit and Bohdan directly. "I hear you two are the best swordsmen this city has to offer. How about this? If you lower your weapons right now, you can work for me instead of being executed along with the rest of these traitors."

"Not going to happen, Sir, sorry." Smit glances at his friend.

"Rot in hell, Mr. Mayor."

"Shame. So be it. Disarm them." He turns to Lady Valtine and smiles. "The city will remain ours my dear."

Valtine opens her mouth to speak but no words come out. A huge clawed hand comes crashing through the window, pulling her screaming into the black night.

"Valtine!" yells the Mayor.

Two Jackals burst through the large windows on the opposite side, their howls filling the room.

"Attack them, fools! Slay them at once!"

The Mayor's men face the Jackals, four against two, fear in their eyes as Rikederf, taking his chance, swings his sword to cut open the cage and pull out the Bogsproggler.

"Soer, Isaac quickly follow me. Smit, Bohdan, cover us."

They run from the hall. Smit and Bohdan slam the heavy wooden doors shut, trapping the Mayor and his men with the Jackals. The Bogsproggler starts squeaking and mumbling, frantically pointing at his wrist and at the doors.

"What is it Bogsproggler?" Soer asks as he continues to squeak and grumble, desperately trying to get his point across.

"Oh no! They can't understand me, I need the bracelet back. What should I do? What should I do?"

The Bogsproggler runs up and down the hallway looking for something that will help. He finds a quill and inkwell atop a dusty table. He jumps up and grabs the quill, knocking the inkwell on to the expensive rug, He dips the quill in the spilt ink and runs back to the group. On the pale oak door, as the Mayor's men shout in fury, he scrawls as fast as he can a drawing of a fireplace and a crude drawing of the bracelet.

"His bracelet, that's what he's after Uncle Rikederf, that's why we can't understand him."

Soer inspects the picture closely. "I think he means it's in the fireplace."

"Smit, don't open this door for anyone but me!" Rikederf slips back into the hall.

The Mayor is waving a small dagger in front of him in a panic as the two remaining guards desperately fend off the last Jackal. The other beast lies motionless next to the bodies of two fallen men. Rikederf runs towards the fireplace, passing the Mayor, knocking him out of the way. His eyes dart left to right, looking for the bracelet, spotting it in the corner, reaching for it to place it safely in his pocket. A sharp pain, cold as ice, pierces his right shoulder. He feels the warm trickle of blood as the truth dawns. Hanismiks' dagger sticks out from his back, but he cannot reach the handle to pull it out. The Mayor grips the hilt, moving it ever so slightly backward and forward and Rikederf winces in pain.

"I think you'll find that belongs to me, hand it over," growls the Mayor

With the fight over, the remaining two men-at-arms stand behind Hanismiks.

Slowly, Rikederf pushes himself back onto the blade, gritting his teeth against the pain. "No."

The two guards suddenly drop to the floor, a gleaming dagger in each of their backs. Startled, the Mayor turns to see Bohdan in the doorway, arms folded and a smug look on his face. The distraction is all Rikederf needs. In one fluid motion, he sidesteps, drawing his sword before the Mayor can react.

"Rikederf," he screams.

The Captain plunges his blade into Hanismiks' stomach. He lets out a faint moan and clings onto Rikederf.

"My father says hello," Rikederf whispers softly into the dying man's ear. "This is his blade, passed down to me after you killed him. I've always known, and now my dear Mayor, you pay the price. Give my regards to your wife."

Hanismiks' eyes fill with surprise and fear. He lets out one last breath, his eyes closing as he falls taking Rikederf with him.

Smit and Bohdan rush to help the Captain up, the dagger still in his shoulder.

Soer enters and examines the wound "It is not serious. I can help him, let's get him back to the barracks."

"I'm fine, I can carry on, I promised this little friend of ours I would get him to the North Gate and that's exactly what I shall do." Rikederf finds his balance and stands tall. "Let's go."

Chapter 11

The North Gate

A beautiful melody fills the sky as the Nin birds descend from the peaks of the Iron Mountains. Bright yellow, pink and orange colour the sky as a new day calls. No more fire, no more clashing of steel and bone, no more howling in the dark. The North Gate is peaceful after a harrowing night, and for once, unmanned in the aftermath of the battle.

The Bogsproggler stands before the gate, his friends behind him.

"Smit, Bohdan, open the gate for our guest here."

"Will do Captain. Bohdan, you take the right."

Smit and Bohdan each take hold of large metal chains on either side of the gate and pull down hard. The massive iron and wooden doors creak open to reveal lush green grass swaying in the wind. A narrow road splits in two, one way leading north to the foothills of the Iron Mountains and disappearing into a tumble of rocks, the other east to the Blue Woods, two days distant. The Bogsproggler hops into the grass and rummages around. Isaac joins his friend and helps him find some small stones covered in moss. Soer and Rikederf walk through the gate to the grassy edge while Smit and Bohdan stand just outside the wall talking and joking like they had the night before.

"Isaac, come here a moment please," Soer says softly.

He strolls over to his mother while Rikederf joins the Bogsproggler.

"Little one, I never thanked you for helping them back in the house. I am eternally grateful."

"It is nothing Mr. Rikederf, sir. I would do anything for my friends."

"And now you have three more."

The Bogsproggler's eyes widen and his face lights up with glee. He hops over to Rikederf and gives him a hug. "Thank you, all of you. Now on to the Blue Woods. I know I must do this last part on my own. You have all done so much for me and I shall never forget it."

"Little one, I shall see to it that Balen-Town lifts its human-only ban, well for most things, not those demons that came in last night, I wonder what they were and why they attacked?"

The Bogsproggler looks up to the captain. "They were Jackals. The things I came across one in the Black Woods,

Brother Blue and Brother Green saved me."

"They were the things you told us about, I thought you said there was only one?"

"That's what I thought."

They both stand for a second looking to the west and can see the Black Woods in the distance over the rooftops.

"Well they are defeated, for now, but we will be ready if they attack again." Rikederf kneels next to his new friend. "Here you go little one, take this."

Squeak grumble. "What is it?"

It's a Bellow Fly. Whenever you need help or are in trouble just throw it up into the air and the Knights of Balen-Town will come to your aid." He places his hand on the Bogsproggler's shoulders, smiles, gets to his feet and walks back to the North Gate.

Smit and Bohdan smile at the Bogsproggler before saluting and taking their leave.

"Thank you, friend." Soer says with gratitude. "If you ever need somewhere to stay, my door is always open." She walks to the Bogsproggler, kisses him once on the cheek and walks back to the gate.

Isaac runs up to the Bogsproggler and hugs him so tight he lets out a little squeak.

"Ha, sorry about that Bogsproggler." They both laugh.

"I'll miss you, Isaac, you're the best friend I've ever had." A tear rolls down his little cheek. Isaac hugs him again.

"I'll miss you too. We shall always be friends, and we shall meet again. I'm going to open a shop that sells all the moss you can eat." They laugh and jump about in the fresh grass.

"Isaac, come on time to go." Soer calls.

Isaac hands the Bogsproggler some more fire paper, hugs him one last time and walks back to the gate.

Everyone gathers together in the gateway. They wave goodbye to their friend as he hops along the road as far as the fork. He turns around and waves back. They wave one last time before Smit and Bohdan step aside and the gate closes.

Alone again, but happy, the Bogsproggler looks up to the bright sun and listens to the beautiful song of the Nin bird. "East is the way I need to go, east to the Blue Woods and then to the cave."

Just as he is about to head down the road to the Blue Woods, something catches his eye along the Iron Mountain trail.

"What was that, not a Jackal?" he squeaks to himself.

His ears prick up. In the distance, he hears something familiar. As fast as his little webbed toes will carry him, he runs up the road towards the Iron Mountains and disappears behind the jagged rocks.

To Be Continued…

Printed in Great Britain
by Amazon